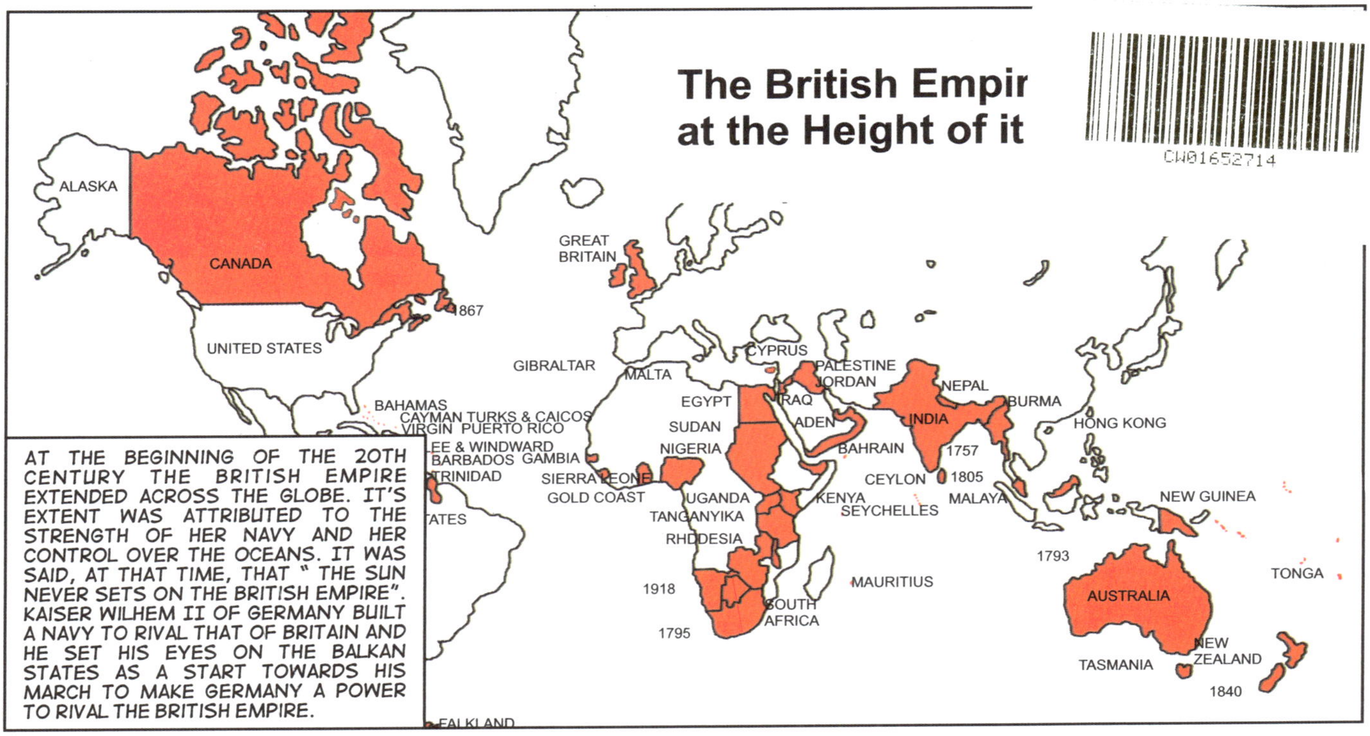

Kaiser Willhelm II

GERMAN MILITARISM UNDER KAISER WILHELM II AFTER 1914 RESULTED IN AN ARMS RACE IN EUROPE CAUSING POLITICAL UNCERTAINTY.

THIS RESULTED IN EUROPEAN POWERS ENTERING INTO ALLIANCES TO PROTECT THEIR NATIONAL INTERESTS. THE TWO MAIN ALLIANCES WERE "THE TRIPLE ENTENTE" OF BRITAIN,FRANCE AND RUSSIA AND THE CENTRAL POWERS CONSISTING OF GERMANY, AUSTRIA, HUNGARY AND ITALY. ALLIES AND COLONIES OF THESE POWERS SUBSEQUENTLY JOINED THE WAR AND FOUGHT ON THE SIDE OF THEIR RESPECTIVE POWERS.

The Assasination of Archduke Ferdinand

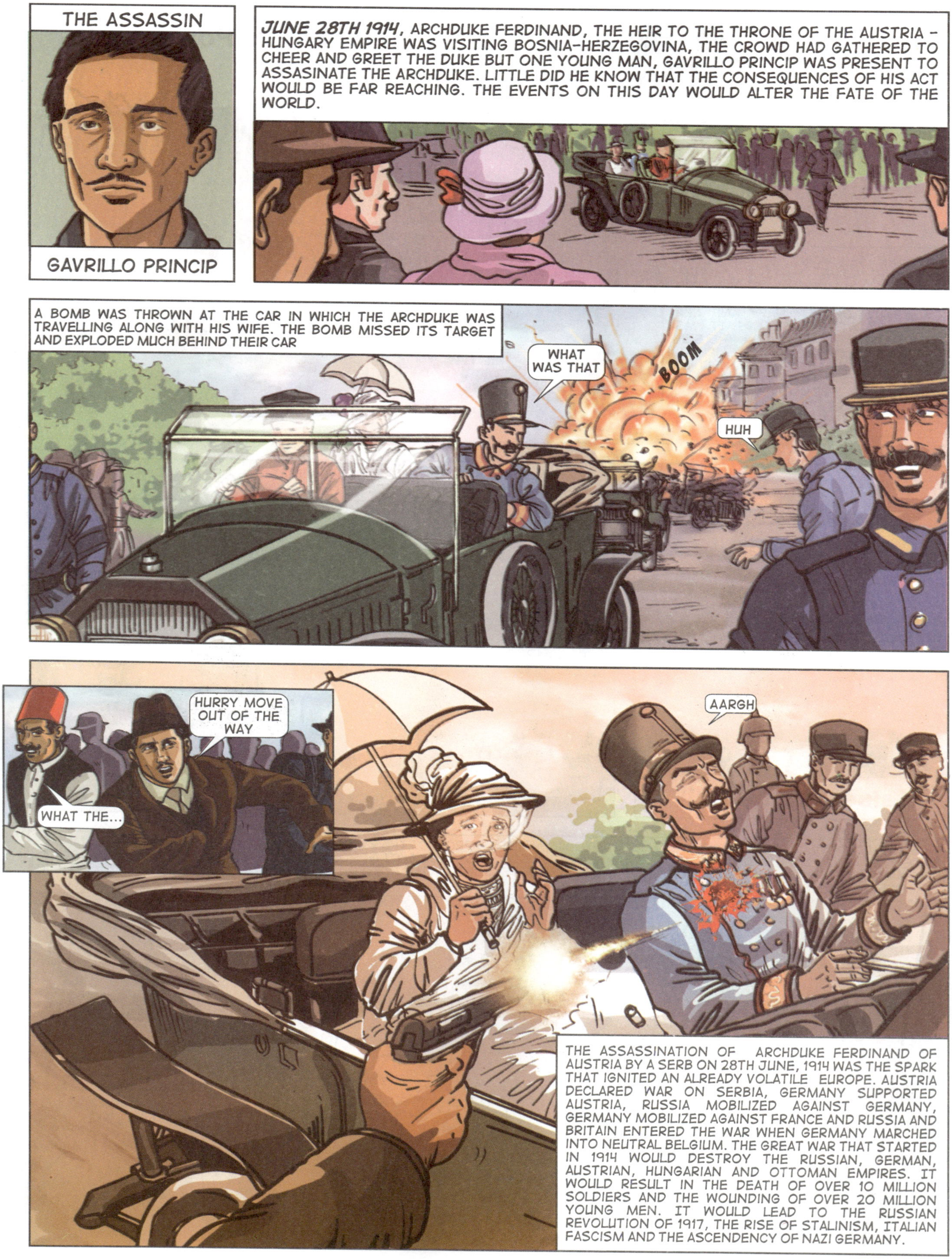

AS PART OF THE BRITISH EMPIRE, INDIA JOINED THE WAR AT THE VERY BEGINNING i.e. IN AUGUST 1914. MAHATMA GANDHI AND SOME OTHER POLITICAL LEADERS WERE OF THE OPINION THAT INDIA'S PARTICIPATION IN THE WAR WOULD LEAD TO SELF-RULE AND FINALLY TO INDEPENDENCE. MAHATMA GANDHI SINGLE HANDEDLY RAISED AN AMBULANCE COMPANY BUT WAS NOT ALLOWED TO PROCEED TO THE FRONT ON ACCOUNT OF ILL-HEALTH. GANDHI HAD TAKEN PART IN THE BOER WAR AS AN AMBULANCE ASSISTANT.

THE INDIAN CORPS CONSISTING OF THE LAHORE AND MEERUT DIVISIONS LANDED AT MARSEILLES IN MID OCTOBER. THEY WERE IN THIN COTTON UNIFORMS ALTHOUGH WINTER WAS SETTING IN. THEY WERE GIVEN THE LEE ENFIELD 303 RIFLE WHICH WAS NEW TO THEM AND PRACTICED FOR A DAY AND SENT TO THE FRONT.

THE 129 BALUCHIS AND THE 57TH (WILDES) RIFLES WERE RUSHED IN BUSES FROM THE RAILHEAD TO THE TRENCHES SOUTH OF YPRES, SPLIT INTO COMPANIES AND USED TO PLUG THE GAPS IN THE LINE HELD BY BRITISH DISMOUNTED CAVALRY. IT IS HERE THAT THE GERMANS CAME NEAREST TO BREAKING THROUGH TO THE CHANNEL PORTS BUT IT WAS THESE UNITS OF THE INDIAN ARMY THAT HELPED TO STOP THEM.

THE BRITISH EXPEDITIONARY FORCE (BEF)- THE "OLD CONTEMPTIBLES"- SO NAMED BY THE KAISER OF GERMANY-WAS ALREADY IN FRANCE AT THE START OF THE WAR TO STOP THE GERMAN ARMY. THEY WERE EXHAUSTED FIGHTING AGAINST A BETTER ARMED GERMAN ARMY WHO WERE ALSO IN OVERWHELMING NUMBERS.

BLIMEY MATES! LOOK WHO IS HERE, ITS OUR REINFORCEMENTS AND ALSO IN THE NICK OF TIME. TALK ABOUT A STROKE OF LUCK!!...
THE BRITISH SECOND CORPS AT THE FIRST BATTLE OF YPRES NEEDED TO BE URGENTLY RELIEVED BUT THERE WERE NO TRAINED BRITISH OR CANADIAN DIVISIONS AVAILABLE. IT WAS THEREFORE DECIDED TO SEND INDIAN TROOPS ALTHOUGH THEY WERE NEITHER EQUIPPED OR TRAINED FOR THIS TYPE OF FIGHTING. INDIAN INFANTRY AND CAVALRY DIVISIONS WERE INDUCTED INTO THE BATTLE ZONE

First Battle of YPRES – 19 Oct to 20 Nov 1914

The Battle of Neuve Chapelle

THERE WERE MANY "FIRSTS" IN THE INTRODUCTION OF NEW WEAPONS IN WORLD WAR I. THESE NEW WEAPONS MADE WAR FIGHTING MORE LETHAL AND TERRIFYING. THEY INCLUDED MACHINE GUNS, POISON GAS, THE TANK, THE AIRPLANE, BARBED WIRE, ANTI-PERSONNEL MINES, THE GRENADE, THE FLAME THROWER AND THE BANGALORE TORPEDO. THE USE OF THESE NEW WEAPONS CAUSED THOUSANDS OF CASUALTIES FOR BOTH THE ALLIED AND AXIS ARMIES.

The Machine Gun

THE MACHINE GUNS WERE OF THREE TYPES LIGHT, MEDIUM AND HEAVY. THE CYCLIC RATE OF FIRE OF THESE MACHINE GUNS OF HUNDREDS OF ROUNDS PER MINUTE AS COMPARED TO THE HAND CONTROLLED BOLT ACTION RIFLE REVOLUTIONIZED WAR FIGHTING. THE MACHINE GUN, WHEN INTERLOCKED WITH OTHER MACHINE GUNS PRODUCED A STEEL WALL OF FIRE DESTROYING ALL WHO ATTEMPTED TO CROSS IT.

Tanks

WITH THE MACHINE GUNS CAUSING SO MUCH DEVASTATION A COUNTER WEAPON PLATFORM HAD TO BE FOUND TO NEUTRALIZE THE LETHALITY OF THE MACHINE GUN. IT WAS THE TANK THAT MET THIS NEED.

THE TANK WAS A VEHICLE THAT WAS HEAVILY ARMORED WHICH WAS IMPERVIOUS TO SMALL ARMS AND MACHINE GUN FIRE. INSTEAD OF WHEELS THE TANK MOVED ON METAL TRACKS THAT ALLOWED IT TO MOVE CROSS-COUNTRY, ACROSS BARBED WIRE ENTANGLEMENTS AND ANTI PERSONNEL MINEFIELDS

Barbed Wire

IN ORDER TO SLOW DOWN ASSAULTING INFANTRY AND TO MAKE IT DIFFICULT FOR THEM TO ASSAULT A DEFENSIVE POSITION BARBED WIRE ENTANGLEMENTS WERE STRUNG ACROSS AND AHEAD OF DEFENSIVE POSITIONS.THE WIRE HAD "BARBS" FIXED ALONG ITS LENGTH THAT TORE INTO THE CLOTHES AND FLESH OF ATTACKING INFANTRY MAKING IT VERY DIFFICULT FOR INFANTRY SOLDIERS TO CROSS THE WIRE OBSTACLE. WHEN USED IN THE FORM OF CONCERTINA COILS THEY MADE THE DEFENSIVE POSITION MORE SECURE AND THAT MUCH MORE DIFFICULT FOR THE ATTACKERS TO NEGOTIATE.

Grenade

THE HAND GRENADE WAS A WEAPON THAT COULD BE USED BY ATTACKERS AS WELL AS DEFENDERS. IT CONSISTED OF A METAL BODY CONTAINING AN EXPLOSIVE AND A FUSE. IT ALSO HAD A LEVER AND A PIN. REMOVAL OF THE PIN AND RELEASE OF THE LEVER ACTUATED THE FUSE WHICH IGNITED THE. EXPLOSIVE SHATTERING THE METAL CONTAINER INTO MANY SPLINTERS CAUSING CASUALTIES AGAINST WHOM THE GRENADE WAS USED.

Jam-Tin Bombs

DURING THE BATTLE OF NEUVE CHAPPELLE THE GARHWALI TROOPS FOUND A HUGE STORE OF BOMBS AND WORKED OUT BY TRIAL AND ERROR HOW TO USE THEM.

INDIAN SAPPERS AND MINERS THEREAFTER TOOK THE LEAD IN THE MANUFACTURE OF JAM-TIN BOMBS

"JAM TIN BOMBS" CONSISTED OF TINS FILLED WITH GUNCOTTON AND NAILS WITH A DETONATOR AND FUSE PUSHED THROUGH THE LID THE FUSE HAD TO BE LIT WITH A CIGARETTE AND THROWN AT THE ENEMY.

Air Craft

DURING WORLD WAR I AIR CRAFT WERE INITIALLY USED AS AIR MOBILE PLATFORMS TO OBSERVE AND REPORT ON THE LOCATION OF ENEMY FORCES AND AS AIR OBSERVATION POSTS TO OBSERVE AND CONTROL ARTILLERY FIRE.

IT WAS ONLY AFTER 1915 THAT THEY WERE USED AS FIGHTERS TO DESTROY ENEMY AIR CRAFT AND AGAINST GROUND FORCES AND ALSO AS BOMBERS.

Poison Gas

THE GERMANS INTRODUCED CHEMICAL WEAPONS IN APRIL 1915 AT THE SECOND BATTLE OF YPRES. DEADLY CHLORINE/MUSTARD GAS WAS RELEASED FROM CONTAINERS WHICH MOVED AS YELLOW CLOUDS CAUSING THE ENEMY DEFENDER TO CHOKE AND DIE. IT ALSO CAUSED BLISTERS ON THE BODY. MANY ALLIED SOLDIERS DIED DUE TO THE EFFECTS OF GAS WARFARE. THE ALLIED FORCES WERE NOT LONG IN USING CHEMICAL WEAPONS AGAINST GERMANY. THE USE OF CHEMICAL WEAPONS IS NOW BANNED BY THE UNITED NATIONS.

Flame Thrower

THE FLAME-THROWER WAS ALSO INTRODUCED BY THE GERMANS DURING WORLD WAR I. THIS WAS A HAND HELD WEAPON THAT WAS FUELLED BY A TANK CONTAINING LIQUID FUEL WHICH FED THE FLAME. THE FLAME BURNT EVERYTHING WITHIN ITS PATH AND WAS USED PARTICULARLY AGAINST ENEMY DEFENSES AND STRONG POINTS.

Bangalore Torpedo

THE BANGALORE TORPEDO, AS THE NAME SUGGESTS, WAS INVENTED BY INDIAN ARMY ENGINEERS. IT WAS PLACED INTO WIRE OBSTACLES AND DETONATED MAKING GAPS IN THE WIRE OBSTACLE.

Artillery

BIG GUNS COULD FIRE AT GREAT DISTANCES AND TO ENGAGE THE ARMY THROUGH DIRECT AND INDIRECT FIRE

The Air War 1914-1918

BOTH BRITAIN AND GERMANY TOOK TIME TO APPRECIATE THE VALUE OF THE AIR ARM. IN THE FIRST MONTH OF THE WAR THE ONLY ROLE ALLOTTED TO AIR CRAFT WAS VISUAL RECONNAISSANCE AND NO PROVISION WAS MADE FOR AERIAL BATTLE OR BOMBING. IN SEPTEMBER 1914 THE ROLE EXTENDED TO OBSERVATION OF TARGETS FOR THE ARTILLERY. IN MARCH 1915 A SPECIAL CAMERA WAS SUPPLIED AND THE VALUE OF AERIAL PHOTOGRAPHY WAS RECOGNIZED AND DEVELOPED. AIRCRAFT WERE EQUIPPED WITH COMMUNICATION SYSTEMS TO COMMUNICATE WITH EACH OTHER AND WITH GROUND TROOPS TO INFORM THEM ABOUT ENEMY MOVEMENT AND BUILD UP. THIS LED TO AIR FIGHTING FOR SUPREMACY OF THE AIR AND ATTACKS ON THE ENEMY GROUND FORCES. BRITISH AND GERMAN PILOTS NOW BEGAN TO FIGHT EACH OTHER IN AERIAL COMBAT AND GUNS WERE DEVELOPED THAT COULD FIRE THROUGH THE ORBIT OF THE REVOLVING PROPELLER WITHOUT RISK OF HITTING THE BLADES. THOSE PILOTS WHO SHOT DOWN MANY OF THE OPPONENTS AIRCRAFT WERE CALLED 'AIR ACES' THE MOST FAMOUS AMONG THEM WAS BARON MANFRED VON RICHTOFEN, BETTER KNOWN AS THE 'RED BARON' HE WAS CALLED THE 'RED BARON' BECAUSE HE HAD HIS AIRCRAFT PAINTED A BRIGHT RED TO BE EASILY RECOGNIZED. HE WAS CREDITED WITH SHOOTING DOWN 80 OF THE OPPONENTS AIRCRAFT BEFORE HE WAS SHOT DOWN HIMSELF.

Lieutenant Indra Lal Roy, DFC
DURING WORLD WAR 1 PILOTS IN THE COMBAT ROLE WERE INITIALLY CALLED 'AVIATORS' AND LATER ON 'SCOUTS' IT WAS MUCH LATER THAT THEY WERE CALLED 'FIGHTER PILOTS' FOUR INDIANS FOUGHT DURING THIS WAR AS FIGHTER PILOTS. TWO WERE KILLED IN COMBAT, ON WAS SHOT DOWN AND TAKEN PRISONER. ONLY ONE SURVIVED. ONLY ONE (INDRANIL ROY) ACHIEVED THE CATEGORY OF BEING CALLED AN AIR ACE AFTER HE DESTROYED 9 GERMAN AIRCRAFT, FOR WHICH HE WAS AWARDED THE DFC
Lieutenant Hardit Singh Malik, OBE, CIE
THE FIRST INDIAN TO FLY IN AERIAL COMBAT WAS HARDIT SINGH MALIK. WHEN WORLD WAR I STARTED HE WAS AT OXFORD UNIVERSITY. HE VOLUNTEERED AND JOINED THE ROYAL FLYING CORPS IN EARLY 1917 AND SAW LOTS OF ACTION SCRAPPING WITH GERMAN FOKKER TRI-PLANES. HE WAS KNOWN AS THE FLYING SIKH OF BIGGIN HILL AND THE INDIAN PEGASUS. HE WAS WOUNDED TWICE AND SHOT DOWN ONCE. HE JOINED THE INDIAN CIVIL SERVICE AFTER THE WAR AND RETIRED IN 1957 AS AMBASSADOR TO FRANCE.

Lieutenant Errol Chunder Sen

WAS BORN IN CALCUTTA BUT EDUCATED IN ENGLAND. HE VOLUNTEERED FOR THE ROYAL FLYING CORPS BUT WAS UNDERAGE AND HAD TO WAIT FOR TWO YEARS AND FINALLY JOINED THE RAF ON 24 APRIL 1917. LIKE MOST PILOTS OF HIS TIME HE FLEW SOPWITH CAMELS ON COMBAT PATROLS OVER FRANCE AND BELGIUM. ON 14 SEP, 1917 HE SHOT DOWN A GERMAN ALBATROSS AND WAS HIMSELF DOWNED NEAR MENIN. HE WAS TAKEN PRISONER AND REMAINED A POW TILL THE ARMISTICE IN NOVEMBER 1918.

Lieutenant S G Wellingkar

AN ALUMNI OF ST. XAVIER'S COLLEGE BOMBAY, HE WAS ADMITTED TO JESUS COLLEGE AT CAMBRIDGE. HE VOLUNTEERED AND JOINED THE ROYAL FLYING CORPS AND GOT HIS WINGS IN APRIL/MAY 1917 AFTER WHICH HE FLEW A NUMBER OF COMBAT SORTIES OVER FRANCE TO BLUNT THE GERMAN OFFENSIVES IN THE SUMMER OF 1918. ON JUNE 27, 1918 HE WAS SHOT DOWN OVER FRANCE AND DIED FROM HIS WOUNDS ON 30 JUNE, 1918.

Assault By Tanks at Cambrai

British Tanks Assaulting German Defences at Cambrai

The Turkish Theatre of Operations

TURKEY ENTERED THE WAR ON 1ST NOVEMBER,1914. TURKEYS APPREHENSION OF BRITISH POWER, HER FEAR OF RUSSIAN INTENTIONS, AGGRESSIVE GERMAN DIPLOMACY AND THE POSSIBILITY OF TURKISH TERRITORIAL GAINS ENCOURAGED HER TO ENTER THE WAR ON THE SIDE OF THE AXIS POWERS.

The Gallipoli Campaign

FRUSTRATED BY THE STALEMATE OF TRENCH WARFARE IN FRANCE, BRITAIN DECIDED TO OPEN A FRONT AGAINST TURKEY. THIS WOULD OFFSET THE DEADLOCK OF THE WAR ON THE WESTERN FRONT AND ALSO OPEN A SUPPLY ROUTE TO SUPPLY HER RUSSIAN ALLY.

THE BRITISH PLAN WAS TO USE HER NAVAL POWER TO FORCE HER WAY THROUGH THE DARDENELLES. THE NAVAL OPERATION HOWEVER WAS A DISASTER AND ITS FAILURE WARNED THE TURKS ABOUT BRITISH INTENTIONS
TURKEY QUICKLY REINFORCED THE AREA WITH SIX DIVISIONS WHILE BRITAIN DELAYED THE OFFENSIVE. BRITAIN'S DELAY HELPED TURKEY TO PREPARE STRONG DEFENSES.
AS A CONSEQUENCE, ALLIED FORCES WERE DECIMATED AT THE LANDING SITES DUE TO THE DIFFICULT TERRAIN AND LACK OF COVER.
INADEQUATE ARTILLERY SUPPORT, POOR MEDICAL SUPPORT, SUBSTANDARD ADMINISTRATION, BRILLIANT STRATEGY BY TURKISH FORCES...
...LED BY GERMAN OFFICERS AND HIGHLY MOTIVATED TURKISH FIGHTERS LED BY COMMITTED TURKISH OFFICERS RESULTED IN THE DEFEAT OF THE BRITISH PLAN TO CAPTURE GALLIPOLI.

INDIA'S 29 INFANTRY BRIGADE INITIALLY CONSISTED OF 14 SIKHS, 69 AND 89 PUNJABIS WHO WERE LATER REPLACED BY 1/5 RGR, 1/6 GR, 2/10 GR AND 1/4 GR SUPPORTED BY TWO INDIAN ARTILLERY MOUNTAIN BATTERIES (21ST KOHAT AND 26TH JACOBS)THE INDIANS FOUGHT ALONGSIDE BRITISH AND ANZAC TROOPS,
AS THE BATTLE RAGED THE TURKS ALSO SUFFERED LOSSES
THE ALLIES TOOK THE BRUNT OF HEAVY CASUALTIES. ALMOST ALL OFFICERS OF THE 29 INDIAN INFANTRY BRIGADE WERE EITHER KILLED OR WOUNDED
THE ALLIED TROOPS CONTINUED THEIR DESPERATE FIGHTING BUT WERE UNABLE TO MAKE ANY BREAKTHROUGH
THE ALLIED TROOPS FOUGHT IN DEPLORABLE CONDITIONS, EXCRUCIATING HEAT LACK OF WATER AND VERY POOR ARTILLERY SUPPORT. THE ALLIES WERE FINALLY FORCED TO WITHDRAW. ALLIED CASUALTIES WERE VERY HEAVY.

The Turkish Theatre of Operations

GENERAL TOWNSHEND MOVED FORWARD IN AUGUST 1915 HE DEFEATED THE TURKS NEAR KUT AND PURSUED THE TURKS TO AZZIZYA HALF WAY TO BAGHDAD.
THE TURKS PUT UP A STRONG DEFENCE AGAINST THE ATTACKING ALLIES
AMBITION GOT THE BETTER OF COMMON SENSE. TOWNSHEND DECIDED TO GO FOR BAGHDAD NOT TAKING INTO ACCOUNT THAT HIS SUPPLY LINE TO KUT ITSELF WAS 180 MILES-TOO LONG BY ANY ESTIMATE. AFTER AN INDECISIVE BATTLE AT CTESIPHON TOWNSHEND RETREATED TO KUT EL-AMARA
THE TURKISH GENERAL NURUDDIN LAID SIEGE TO HIS FORCE AT KUT TOWNSHEND HAD WITH HIM THE 24TH AND 66TH PUNJABIS, 2/7 GURKHAS, 17 MARATHAS. THE SIEGE LASTED FROM 15 DECEMBER 1915 UP TO 29TH APRIL 2016 UNDER APPALLING CONDITIONS. THOUSANDS OF INDIAN SOLDIERS PERISHED DUE TO LACK OF FOOD, WATER AND MEDICAL SUPPORT DURING THE SIEGE, SUBSEQUENTLY THE GARRISON SURRENDERED TO THE TURKS.
FINALLY, GENERAL SIR STANLEY MAUDE TOOK BACK MESOPOTAMIA ONCE AGAIN WITH INDIAN TROOPS CONSISTING OF SIKHS, MARATHA AND GURKHAS ASSISTED BY THE MADRAS AND BENGAL SAPPERS. THE HIGHEST CASUALTIES OF INDIAN TROOPS IN WORLD WAR I OCCURRED AT MESOPOTAMIA INCLUDING OVER 30,000 DEAD AND 32,000 WOUNDED. THE CAMPAIGN WHICH HOPED TO OFFSET THE REVERSE AT GALLIPOLI ITSELF PROVED TO BE A DISASTER.

The Palestine Campaign 1918
INDIAN TROOPS PLAYED A MAJOR ROLE IN THE CAMPAIGNS IN TURKEY AND PALESTINE THE PALESTINE CAMPAIGN HOWEVER WAS A REFRESHING CHANGE FROM THE MISMANAGEMENT AND DISASTER AT GALLIPOLI AND MESOPOTAMIA. THE TURKISH ARMIES WERE LED BY THE GERMAN GENERAL LEMAN VON SANDERS AND THE ALLIES WERE LED BY SIR EDMUND ALLENBY, BUT IT WAS BETTER LEADERSHIP, SUPERIOR STRATEGY, FLEXIBLE TACTICS AND GOOD ADMINISTRATION OF THE ALLIES THAT WON THE DAY.
Edmund Allenby
Liman von Sanders
ALTHOUGH IT WAS INDIAN INFANTRY THAT INITIALLY BROKE THROUGH THE TURKISH DEFENSES IT WAS THE INDIAN CAVALRY THAT PUSHED THROUGH THE GAP THAT TURNED THE BRITISH SUCCESS INTO A TURKISH ROUT IN WHAT HAS COME TO BE KNOWN AS THE BATTLE OF MEGIDDO. THE 7TH INDIAN (MEERUT) DIVISION FROM MESOPOTAMIA AND THE INDIAN CAVALRY CORPS FROM FRANCE WERE MOVED TO PALESTINE KEEPING IN MIND THEIR CAPACITY TO PERFORM BETTER IN TERRAIN, CLIMATE AND A ROLE MORE SUITABLE TO THEIR CAPABILITY AND POTENTIAL.
GENERAL ALLENBY SPENT VALUABLE TIME TRAINING HIS DESERT MOUNTED CORPS WHICH INCLUDED THE 4TH AND 5TH INDIAN CAVALRY DIVISIONS AND WORKING OUT AN INTRICATE DECEPTION PLAN THAT CONFUSED THE TURKS AS TO THE TIME AND PLACE FROM WHERE HE WOULD ATTACK.
ORDER OF BATTLE OF 4TH AND 5TH INDIAN CAVALRY DIVISION INCLUDED THE FOLLOWING INDIAN CAVALRY UNITS
2ND LANCERS
CENTRAL INDIA HOUSE
SCINDE HORSE
29TH LANCERS
19TH LANCERS
HODSON'S HORSE
POONA HORSE
18THLANCERS
DECCAN HORSE
JODHPUR LANCERS
MYSORE LANCERS
HYDERABAD LANCERS
6TH CAVALRY

General Allenby's Strategy

THOMAS EDWARD LAWRENCE, CB, DSO WAS A BRITISH ARMY OFFICER RENOWNED ESPECIALLY FOR HIS LIAISON ROLE DURING THE SINAI AND PALESTINE CAMPAIGN, AND THE ARAB REVOLT AGAINST OTTOMAN TURKISH RULE OF 1916-18. THE BREADTH AND VARIETY OF HIS ACTIVITIES AND ASSOCIATIONS, AND HIS ABILITY TO DESCRIBE THEM VIVIDLY IN WRITING EARNED HIM INTERNATIONAL FAME AS LAWRENCE OF ARABIA.

HIS MAJOR CONTRIBUTION TO THE REVOLT WAS CONVINCING THE ARAB LEADERS TO CO-ORDINATE THEIR ACTIONS IN SUPPORT OF BRITISH STRATEGY.

Lawrence of Arabia

HE ALSO USED THE AIR FORCE TO BOMB THE TURKISH HEADQUARTERS AND THE RETREATING TURKISH ARMY. DERAA, EL AFULE AND BEISAN WERE STRATEGIC OBJECTIVES IN THE TURKISH REAR. THEIR CAPTURE WOULD ENSURE THE COLLAPSE OF THE TURKS. THE OFFENSIVE WHICH COMMENCED ON 19TH SEPTEMBER, 1918 WENT EXACTLY ACCORDING TO PLAN. THE CONVERGENCE OF TURKISH ROAD AND RAIL COMMUNICATION AT DERAA, EL AFULE AND BEISAN MADE THE CAPTURE OF THESE LOCATIONS CRITICAL TO THE SUCCESS OF THE ALLIED PLAN. ALLENBY USED THE INFANTRY TO BREAK THROUGH THE TURKISH DEFENSES THAT GUARDED THESE THREE STRATEGIC LOCATIONS AND HIS MOUNTED FORCES- MAINLY INDIAN CAVALRY TO SURGE THROUGH AND TO CAPTURE THESE STRATEGIC LOCATIONS IN THE REAR OF THE TURKISH DEFENSES.

The Battle of Megiddo

THE INDIAN CAVALRY CHARGE LED BY JODHPUR LANCERS – "THE LAST CAVALRY CHARGE IN MILITARY HISTORY".

Campaign in East Africa

GERMAN AMBITIONS FOR A LARGER SHARE OF COLONIES IN AFRICA AND ASIA WAS ONE OF THE CAUSES THAT LEAD TO THE GREAT WAR. THIS RIVALRY BETWEEN GERMANY AND BRITAIN EXTENDED THE WAR INTO THE COLONIES IN AFRICA AND ASIA. GERMANY HOWEVER BY THE END OF THE WAR LOST WHATEVER GERMANY POSSESSED BEFORE THE ONSET OF WORLD WAR I. BRITAIN, FRANCE, SOUTH AFRICA, AUSTRALIA AND NEW ZEALAND ALL ADDED TO THEIR COLONIES WHAT WAS POSSESSED BY GERMANY.

GERMAN FORCES IN EAST AFRICA WERE COMMANDED BY LIEUTENANT COLONEL PAUL VON LETTOW-VORBECK WHO CONDUCTED A SKILLFUL GUERILLA CAMPAIGN AGAINST THE ALLIES. ALTHOUGH SMALLER IN SIZE. HIS FORCES HELD ON THROUGHOUT THE WAR, SURRENDERING ONLY AFTER THE ARMISTICE OF 11 NOVEMBER 1918.

Battles of Tanga

THE INITIAL BATTLE FOR THE PORT OF TANGA WAS UNSUCCESSFUL AND THE INDIAN FORCE FARED BADLY IN NOVEMBER 1914.

A BATTALION OF THE KASHMIR RIFLES WAS THE ONLY UNIT TO ACHIEVE SOME SUCCESS. THEY CAPTURED TWO LINES OF TRENCHES AND REACHED THE OUTSKIRTS OF TANGA AND COVERED THE WITHDRAWAL OF THE MAIN FORCE.

SUBSEQUENTLY THE 40TH PATHANS AND THE 129TH BALUCH UNDER GENERAL SMUTS WERE SUCCESSFUL AND TANGA WAS FINALLY CAPTURED AFTER FEBRUARY 1917.

The Capture of the Ports of Kilwa and Kilbata

GENERAL SMUTS APPRECIATED THE ADVANTAGES THAT THE GERMANS HAD WITH REGARD TO COMMUNICATION AND OF GUERILLA WARFARE IN INHOSPITABLE TERRAIN. SO HE SPEEDED UP THE ADVANCE ON LAND BY OUTFLANKING THE ENEMY BY SEA IN A SERIES OF LEFT HOOKS FROM ONE SMALL PORT TO ANOTHER. IN THIS MANNER KILWA WAS CAPTURED BY 40TH PATHANS AND THE 129TH BALUCHIS AND THE KINGS AFRICAN RIFLES ON 16 OCTOBER 1916 AND KILBATA THEREAFTER. THE INDIAN INFANTRY UNITS WERE SUPPORTED BY THE DERA JAT MOUNTAIN BATTERY.

DIFFICULTIES FACED BY INDIAN FORCES

- VAST EXTENT OF OPERATIONS
- RAMPANT DISEASES INCLUDING MALARIA, TICK TYPHUS, DYSENTERY BLACK WATER FEVER, JAUNDICE, SLEEPING SICKNESS WHICH TOOK A HEAVY TOLL ON INDIAN TROOPS
- GOOD LINES OF COMMUNICATIONS FOR THE GERMANS TILL THE ALLIES TOOK OVER THE RAILWAY
- BRILLIANT GUERILLA WARFARE BY VORBECK'S FORCES

Hospitals for Indian Solders

DUE TO THE LARGE NUMBER OF CASUALTIES, HOSPITALS IN FRANCE AND BELGIUM COULD NOT COPE WITH THE EVER INCREASING CASUALTIES. THIS LED TO TEMPORARY HOSPITALS BEING ESTABLISHED IN ENGLAND. ONE PARTICULAR HOSPITAL WAS THE HOSPITAL AT BRIGHTON WHICH SPECIFICALLY LOOKED AFTER INDIAN SOLDIERS FIGHTING ON THE WESTERN FRONT. THE BRIGHTON PAVILION WAS CONVERTED INTO A HOSPITAL WITH AN OPERATION THEATRE, X-RAY DEPARTMENT, KITCHENS AND OTHER FACILITIES. SIGNS THROUGHOUT THE HOSPITAL WERE PRINTED IN URDU, HINDI AND GURMUKHI. THE HOSPITAL HAD 724 BEDS AND IT LOOKED AFTER 4,306 WOUNDED INDIAN SOLDIERS. THOSE WHO DIED IN THE HOSPITAL WERE CREMATED OR BURIED ACCORDING TO THEIR RELIGIOUS DENOMINATION.

The Contribution of India's Princely States to World War

THE PRINCELY STATES OF INDIA ENTRENCHED IN MARTIAL PRACTICE AND WELL VERSED IN W
TO PRACTICE THEIR HEROIC TRADITION AND CAPACITY FOR WAR FIGHTING. THEY SUPPORT
BATTALIONS, A CAMEL CORPS, SAPPERS AND MINERS, COMMUNICATION AND TRANSPORT FR
FORCE THAT DELIVERED THE COUPDE GRACE THAT TERMINATED THE WAR IN PALESTINE A
MESOPOTAMIA, SALONICA, PERSIA, PALESTINE AND SYRIA. THE DECORATIONS THAT TH

Maharajah Ganga Singh of Bikaner

CAVALRY	INFANTRY	CAMEL COR
ALWAR LANCERS	1ST ALWAR	BIKANER
BHOPAL LANCERS	3RD GWALIOR	BHAWALPUR
GWALIOR LANCERS	4TH GWALIOR	MOUNTED
HYDERABAD LANCERS	1ST KASHMIR	ESCORT
JODHPUR LANCERS	2ND KASHMIR	KHAISPUR
PATIALA LANCERS	3RD KASHMIR	MOUNTED
MYSORE LANCERS	BHARATPUR	ESCORT
RAMPUR LANCERS	JIND	SAPPERS & MINERS
BHAVNAGAR LANCERS	KAPURTHALA	MINERS
KASHMIRI LANCERS	NABHA	FARIDKOTE
NAWANAGAR LANCERS	1ST PATIALA	MALERKOTLA
JUNAGADH LANCERS	2ND PATIALA	SIRMOOR
UDAIPUR LANCERS	BHOPAL	TEHRI GARHWAL
INDORE MOUNTED ESCORT	BIKANER	
	KHAIRPUR	

HTING SUPPORTED THE WAR WITH GREAT ENTHUSIASM. IT OFFERED THEM AN OPPORTUNITY
TAIN'S WAR WITH MEN, ANIMALS, MONEY AND MATERIAL, WITH CAVALRY UNITS, INFANTRY
E INCEPTION OF THE WAR TO ITS GRAND FINALE WHEN ITS CAVALRY UNITS WERE PART OF THE
RIA, THEY FOUGHT WITH DISTINCTION AT SUEZ, EGYPT, EAST AFRICA, FRANCE, GALLIPOLI,
CEIVED ARE A TESTIMONY TO THEIR CHARACTER AND CONDUCT IN WAR.

ARTILLERY	**HONOURS& AWARDS**
1ST KASHMIR MTN BTY	KBE-1
	DSO-1
2ND KASHMIR MTN BTY	MBE-2
	CIE-7
SIGNALS	MC-15
	OBE 1ST CLASS 36
JANJIRA	OBE 2ND CLASS72
TRANSPORT CORPS UNITS FROM:	1DSM 300
JAIPUR	LEGION OF HONOUR 1
MYSORE	CROIXDE GUERRA-9
BHAWALPUR	ORDER OF THE NILE-3
BHARATPUR	SERBIAN GOLD MEDAL 3
GWALIOR	SERBIAN SILVER MEDAL 3
INDORE	CROSS OF ST GEORGE 5
	ORDER OF ST. STANISLAUS-1

Maharajah Bhupinder Singh of Patiala

Honouring India's War Dead of World War I

THE MEMORY OF INDIANS WHO DIED IN WORLD WAR I HAS BEEN COMMEMORATED WITH HONOUR BY MEMORIALS AROUND THE WORLD. THE PRINCIPAL ONES AMONG THESE ARE INDIA GATE AT NEW DELHI AND NEUVE CHAPELLE IN FRANCE.

India Gate – New Delhi, India

INSCRIPTION ON INDIA GATE

"TO THE DEAD OF THE INDIAN ARMIES WHO FELL AND ARE HONOURED IN FRANCE AND FLANDERS, MESOPOTAMIA AND PERSIA, EAST AFRICA, GALLIPOLI AND IN THE NEAR AND FAR EAST AND IN SACRED MEMORY OF THOSE NAMES ARE HERE RECORDED AND WHO FELL IN INDIA AND THE NORTH WEST FRONTIER AND DURING THE THIRD AFGHAN WAR"

Neuve Chapelle Memorial

THE NEUVE CHAPELLE MEMORIAL IS DEDICATED TO THE INDIAN SOLDIERS WHO LAID DOWN THEIR LIVES IN FRANCE & BELGIUM FROM 1914–1918.

Menin Gate Memorial

Teen Murti Memorial

TEEN MURTI (LITERALLY "THREE STATUES") MEMORIAL BY BRITISH SCULPTOR, LEONARD JENNINGS, WHICH STANDS ON THE ROAD JUNCTION IN FRONT OF ITS EXTENSIVE GROUNDS. THE MEMORIAL COMPRISES LIFE-SIZE STATUES OF THREE SOLDIERS, AND WAS BUILT IN 1922 IN MEMORY OF THE INDIAN SOLDIERS FROM THREE INDIAN PRINCELY STATES, NAMELY; JODHPUR STATE, HYDERABAD STATE AND MYSORE STATE.

1.TOWARDS THE END OF 1918, GERMANY AND THE CENTRAL POWERS, BEATEN AND EXHAUSTED, SUED FOR PEACE AND SIGNED AN ARMISTICE AT VERSAILLES WHICH INCORPORATED MASSIVE PUNITIVE TERMS.

2. THE POLITICAL RAMIFICATIONS OF WORLD WAR I LED TO THE RUSSIAN REVOLUTION OF 1917, FASCISM IN ITALY, NAZISM IN GERMANY, DEEPENING OF TENSIONS BETWEEN CHINA AND JAPAN AND BROUGHT AMERICA INTO THE WAR GIVING HER THE OPPORTUNITY AND SPACE TO EXERCISE GLOBAL HEGEMONY. IT ALSO SET INDIA ON THE PATH TO FREEDOM AND THE INSTITUTION OF THE LEAGUE OF NATIONS.

3. THE AFTERMATH OF THE WAR RESULTED IN THE DECIMATION OF FOUR MULTI-ETHNIC EMPIRES - THE RUSSIAN EMPIRE, THE OTTOMAN EMPIRE, THE AUSTRIA - HUNGARIAN EMPIRE AND THE BRITISH EMPIRE..

4.10 MILLION YOUNG MEN WERE KILLED AND MORE THAN 20 MILLION WERE WOUNDED, MANY OF THEM DISABLED FOR LIFE.

In Flanders Fields

In Flanders fields the poppies blow
Between the crosses, row on row,
That mark our place; and in the sky
The larks, still bravely singing, fly
Scarce heard amid the guns below.

We are the Dead. Short days ago
We lived, felt dawn, saw sunset glow,
Loved and were loved, and now we lie
In Flanders fields

Take up our quarrel with the foe:
To you from failing hands we throw
The torch; be yours to hold it high.
If ye break faith with us who die
We shall not sleep, though poppies grow
In Flanders fields.

John McCrae